THIS WALKER BOOK BELONGS TO:

_____

_____

_____

_____

To Tom and Maddy

First published 1992 by Walker Books Ltd
87 Vauxhall Walk, London SE11 5HJ

This edition published 1999

2 4 6 8 10 9 7 5 3 1

© 1992 Catherine and Laurence Anholt

This book has been typeset in Veronan Light Educational.

Printed in Hong Kong

British Library Cataloguing in Publication Data
A catalogue record for this book is
available from the British Library.

ISBN 0-7445-6746-7 (hb)
ISBN 0-7445-6068-3 (pb)

THE TWINS
TWO BY TWO

Catherine and Laurence Anholt

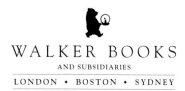

WALKER BOOKS
AND SUBSIDIARIES
LONDON • BOSTON • SYDNEY

Minnie and Max were
having a bedtime story.
It was about Noah's Ark
and all the animals.

"Now it's off to bed two
by two," said Mummy.

On the stairs the twins
were tigers . . .

and in the bathroom they splashed like crocodiles.

"You sound like two noisy elephants," said Mummy when she came up.

"We're not elephants,
we're two little monkeys,"
said Minnie.

"You certainly are," said
Mummy, tucking them
into bed.

In the dark, the twins were two bats flying.

Then they jumped about like kangaroos.

There was so much noise
that Daddy came up.
But where were the twins?

"We're two little bears,"
said a voice from under
the blankets.

Daddy put one little bear
back in his own bed.

But soon Minnie heard
Max crying.

"There's a lion under my
bed," he sniffed.

Minnie was very brave.
She looked under Max's
bed. It wasn't a lion.

It was Ginger!

The twins curled up
together and closed
their eyes.

"We're two little mice,"
they whispered – then fell
fast asleep.

MORE WALKER PAPERBACKS
For You to Enjoy

Also by Laurence and Catherine Anholt

WHAT I LIKE

"Children's likes and dislikes, as seen by six children but with a universality which makes them appealing to all… The scant, rhyming text is elegantly fleshed out by delicate illustrations full of tiny details." *Children's Books of the Year*

0-7445-6070-5   £4.99

WHAT MAKES ME HAPPY?

"This lively book explores children's different emotions, through their own eyes, using simple rhymes and evocative illustrations."
Mother and Baby

0-7445-6069-1   £4.99

KIDS

"From the absurd to the ridiculous, from the real to the imaginary, from the nasty to the charming, this is a book which touches on the important aspects of life as experienced by the young child." *Books for Keeps*

0-7445-6067-5   £4.99

HERE COME THE BABIES

"Over 70 warm and funny pictures of babies to amuse and entertain – especially those with a younger brother or sister." *Practical Parenting*

0-7445-6066-7   £4.99